CW00376477

CLAIMING HIS VIRGIN

INTERSTELLAR BRIDES® PROGRAM: THE
VIRGINS - 3

GRACE GOODWIN

GET A FREE BOOK!

JOIN MY MAILING LIST TO BE THE FIRST TO KNOW OF NEW
RELEASES, FREE BOOKS, SPECIAL PRICES AND OTHER
AUTHOR GIVEAWAYS.

http://freescifiromance.com

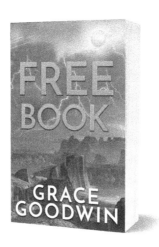

INTERSTELLAR BRIDES® PROGRAM

YOUR mate is out there. Take the test today and discover your perfect match. Are you ready for a sexy alien mate (or two)?

VOLUNTEER NOW!
interstellarbridesprogram.com

*H*elen, *Planet Everis, the Touchstone*

I ENTERED THE BEAUTIFUL GARDEN, MY KNEES WEAK. I followed the path as instructed and found the beautiful white stone bench exactly where he'd promised: next to a bubbling fountain and surrounded by flowers. Their sweet scent filled the air, and I felt like I was living in a fairy tale.

The most unusual fairy tale that involved a little *Star Trek* and a strange bit of palm tingling.

Why? This wasn't a garden in the Virginia town I grew up in. No, I volunteered to be an Interstellar Bride and traveled light years across the galaxy to meet *him*, my one true match. My mate. My *Marked* Mate. I

ran my fingers over my palm where my birthmark—
no, my mark—pulsed and almost burned in reminder
that he was near.

After the transport and the meetings, visiting with
the other women who'd arrived at the Touchstone to
find their mate, I still didn't have any answers. But as I
stared at the thick strip of black silk draped with such
care over the bench, I dared to hope. Hope that he
would understand. Hope that he would know exactly
what I needed. Had Warden Egara—the woman who'd
conducted the testing at the center in Miami—been
correct and the Brides Program's test had tapped into
my subconscious needs? Things I wanted and could
never say aloud? They were too…dark, too
embarrassing.

I lifted the black silk into my hands, felt the cool
slide of the material, and I was shocked to discover that
my fingers shook. My heart pounded, fluttered so fast.
I couldn't count the beats, could barely breathe. This
was it.

The moment.

What I held in my hand was everything I wanted.
Strange, it being a blindfold, but he'd promised me in
the dream if I put it on, he'd give me the world. No, the
entire galaxy. Insane, doing what a man in a dream had
told me, but it was *him.*

I'd been told only Marked Mates would dream
share. Only Marked Mates would have the marks on

their palms awaken. That it was a true gift because only a small number found their other half.

I had. A woman from Earth who somehow was an Everian descendent. The mark on my palm proved it. The other women gave me looks of envy that my mark had awakened so quickly, that *he* was close. Here.

I bit my lip, tried to stifle the nervous smile that turned my lips.

Unable to stand for another moment, I turned and sat down on the bench. The chill of the stone reached through the diaphanous white gown I wore. But even the cold was not enough to shock me from my nervous anticipation of what was to come. No, of *who* was to come.

On Earth, I was considered a broken woman. Strange. Caught in the past even. Especially in the city where I was raised, where women wore power suits, three-inch heels, and college degrees like badges of honor. I was supposed to be confident, aggressive, demanding. I was supposed to want true equality between the sexes. Demand it. But I wanted none of those things. The truth of the matter was I spent most of my life feeling afraid, vulnerable, and weak. I didn't want to be strong. I wanted to serve. I found peace in giving to others. Comfort.

My grandmother had been like that, content in raising her four children, happily greeting my grandfather at the door when he came home from work. Making casseroles for neighbors in need. The white picket fence. Kissing booboos. She hadn't wanted a career outside the home, outside of the life with her husband. I wanted that, too. But on Earth I was about fifty years too late in my thoughts.

I wanted to find a man strong enough to take care of me, to make me feel safe. Cherished.

My desires made me an outcast among my peers. Twenty-three and a college graduate, I was supposed to be something I simply was not. I was smart enough to know my own mind, and I had no desire to rule the world. I was a professional photographer, and a good one. I worked with fashion models and actresses, industry icons who played with men like they'd play with their dolls. Using them in a desperate attempt to rule the world before their beauty faded, their fifteen minutes of fame was over.

The only thing I wanted was a man strong enough to rule me.

Yes, rule. Maybe being light years away from Earth finally gave me the courage to even think that. I couldn't go back—there was no returning once matched—so I could let those thoughts overwhelm me. I could be the real me, to go after what I wanted.

Shuddering now, I could feel his eyes on me. Somehow, I knew he watched me struggle to make this decision. For if I put the blindfold over my eyes, he would come for me. He would take me from this beautiful place and conquer my body. He'd already conquered my soul. My hope.

4

In the dreams we shared, he'd promised me pleasure. I shivered, remembering the deep gravelly tone of his voice, the dominance of his touch. It made him impossible to resist. I looked down in my lap at the thick strip of silk spread across my knees and made my decision. No, I'd already made it. I'd just needed a minute to just…breathe. I hadn't come halfway across the galaxy to lose my courage now. I wasn't afraid of him in the dreams, and I wasn't afraid of him now.

All I had to do was put the blindfold on and everything I ever wanted would happen.

Taking a deep breath, I lifted the strip of silk and covered my eyes completely, tied a firm knot at the back of my head. I could see nothing, the fabric blocking out almost all light except for a thin sliver at the bottom. As instructed, I folded my hands together demurely and sat with my spine straight and my head bent, waiting for my master to come claim me.

A little nervous laugh escaped my lips. My heart fluttered like the wings of a butterfly.

Yes, master. He would be in charge. In control. He would love me with a guiding hand—and perhaps a firm one, too. I ached for that. For him. If he watched, he'd see my nipples hard against my thin gown. They ached with the need to be touched, suckled.

I wanted this.

I wanted him.

He didn't make me wait long. It was as if I could feel him, his body, his desire coming closer. I held my breath when I heard the slightest scruff of footsteps on the path.

"You are so beautiful."

I knew that voice, felt it all the way to my bones. The rough timbre of it was even more seductive in person than in the dreams we shared, and my entire body shivered in response. Goose bumps rose on my arms, yet I wasn't the least bit cold. I bit my lip and didn't respond as he'd not asked me to. I waited impatiently for him to touch me, and when it finally came, my entire body melted. I gasped as his huge, warm hand came to rest at the back base of my neck. I startled, then calmed as his thumb gently massaged the knots he found there.

All at once, I felt his power in the gentle, yet firm, grasp.

The other brides at the Touchstone—the meeting place for those interested in finding a mate from the new arrivals through the testing program—had fussed over me this morning, when I had finally told them about the dreams. They'd been excited—and envious—for me that my match was here, the dreams the first sign of his proximity. They'd spent hours putting my hair up in an elaborate braid that left my neck and shoulders bare. The dress I wore covered one shoulder and dipped low off the other, leaving it exposed. The material was thin and clung to every curve. I had plenty, perhaps too many. I wasn't a waif like the models I photographed. Far from it. But this dress was lovely, even on me. The color, the pale white of freshly fallen snow, I wore at his request. It was easy to do as he wished, for his pleasure was my pleasure. The lack of undergarments was my choice though. I wanted him to see how badly I needed him, that I offered myself to him completely. I didn't want to hide.

I wanted him to know when my nipples hardened, when my breath caught in my throat. That when my dress was pooled at my feet, there was only me and every inch of me belonged to him. And I wanted something else.

"What is your name?" I asked, my curiosity winning out on protocol.

He'd come to me three nights in a row, in my dreams. Every night I'd been at the Touchstone, on Everis. And all three times, he'd asked me to close my eyes. To trust.

His fingers squeezed slightly, prompting me to his dominance. "You will call me Master and nothing else."

The words made me shiver, made my pussy clench, made me wet, my body drowning in heat.

I licked my suddenly dry lips. "Yes, Master."

"Good little mate."

While he kept one hand at my nape, the touch of his fingers of the other was featherlight as he traced the intricate lines of my braids, the seam of my gown. The curve of my lips, exploring me as if I were the finest china and might break at the softest touch. I barely breathed as he took his time.

"Are you ready to come with me?"

Was I ready? "Yes," I replied, almost a groan. *Yes* to everything. I wanted it all.

"Never lie to me. Never deceive me. You must always be honest about what you feel and what you need. Do you understand?" He moved and I heard him settle before me. I could hear his breathing, knew his face was directly before mine which meant he was kneeling. He took hold of both of my hands in his much larger ones. My mark pulsed and throbbed, seemingly knowing its match had finally made contact. I couldn't see him, but I felt his breath. And even though we'd never been this close physically before, I breathed in his familiar scent. How was it possible it was familiar and yet we'd never met? I wished in that moment to rip the blindfold from my eyes and see the Hunter before me. To leap into his arms, to tuck my face into his neck, breathe him in, kiss him there. *Lick* him.

I could do it. Just lift my hands, tug down the silk. Others would do so, but I wouldn't give in to temptation. I'd chosen this path. Him. And this was how we both wanted it. Seeing him was not my choice, but his. I had to hope that one day he would trust me enough to let me see him, deem me worthy. For now, I was content to be what he wanted. To obey. To trust.

"Yes, I am ready."

"You must understand completely," he replied. "If

you are mine, and you disobey me in this, you will be punished, mate."

The thought sent a thrill down my spine. "What do you mean? How will you punish me?" My mind raced with possibilities, but I could settle on none of them. I wasn't a child to be punished. And if he got too weird or overbearing, well, there were other fish in the sea. Lots of other fish. The problem was, I didn't want them. I wanted *him.* My master.

His big hands stroked the outside of my thighs, the large palms firm and hot through the thin material of my gown. "I will lay you over my lap and spank your bare bottom until you beg for forgiveness. Until every touch of my palm spreads like fire. Until you are consumed with it."

Holy shit. I should be freaking out at the idea of being spanked. Spanked! But no, I was definitely broken because my pussy clenched and I imagined myself naked, spread over his lap, both my ass and pussy on display for him to…master. Spank. Fuck.

"Yes, Master."

Gods, yes. Maybe I could start with a little white lie right now and see what happened…No. No. No! What was *wrong* with me? This man had me twisted up in knots. In the possibility of what we would be together.

"I may be the one in control, but you have all the power. One word, Helen, one word from those full lips of yours and everything will stop. Do you understand?"

He reminded me of the conversation we'd had in

the dream the night before, when I agreed to meet him. I knew what he was talking about, this one word. On Earth, it was a safe word. But I didn't want to be safe. I just wanted him and so I nodded.

His large hands cradled mine in my lap once again, his thumbs gently rubbed the palms, sending tingles in a hundred different directions at once. Scattering my thoughts as well.

"What is this word? What is the one utterance that always makes everything stop? What is the word that makes you the master and me your willing slave?"

I didn't want anything to stop. Not now that we'd just begun. Not now that he was before me. Finally. I wanted everything he would give me. While I was nervous, I was confident he *knew* exactly what I needed, perhaps better than I did myself. The flare of heat from the mark was my belief in that. We'd been destined for just this moment.

But I gave him this, because he asked. Because it was all I had to give him at the moment. I licked my lips and said, "Butterfly."

I chose the word because it was one I would never utter accidentally—were there even butterflies on Everis?—and because it represented this journey I was on, my transformation from scared and alone to being claimed. Useful. Protected. I felt like I was about to emerge from my chrysalis and become something more, something I never dared let myself be on Earth. Butterfly represented the risk I took traveling halfway across the galaxy. For him. For myself.

Warden Egara had promised me, when she'd processed me back on Earth, this match would be perfect. That the Coalition had been doing this for hundreds of years, even though Earth matches had been happening for only a short time. That the test never failed.

I chose to believe her, and my mark.

"Butterfly. Come then." He stirred and took my hands, gently leading me I knew not where, but I had only taken a few steps when he swept me up into his arms. I gasped at the ease with which he held me as he carried me the rest of the way to…somewhere. He was so warm, so hard. So big. I relaxed in his hold, unknowing and uncaring where we might be going. Perhaps it was insanity. I could hear the voices from my past yelling at me, advising caution. To go off with a stranger, blindfolded. But I was beyond all that. This wasn't Earth. The rules here were different. None of my friends at home had been tested. None of my friends back home had a mark that led them to their one true match. I wasn't afraid, not with him. He was mine. I knew it, I knew it in the depths of my soul. And when we touched, when we shared dreams, this strange mark that I had believed a birthmark all these years heated on my palm as if I'd been burned by an iron. It proved it all. And so I smiled. Ready.

According to Officiate Treva, who was in charge of

all the brides who arrived on Everis, the burning and dream sharing meant he was my Marked Mate, my perfect match, a one in a hundred chance. Hunters who'd served honorably in the Coalition Fleet and had earned an Interstellar Bride sometimes didn't find their Marked Mate. But mine had. *I* had. I'd dream shared starting the first night and my mark had heated as soon as I woke up from transport.

Warden Egara's testing seemed irrelevant if the mark on my palm matched me to him, if it proved he was nearby. But it had led me here, to him. Without the testing, I'd never have known it wasn't a birthmark, that it was so much more.

He'd found me. Come to me in my dreams and now in person. He carried me away to claim me.

He held me as if I weighed nothing, the steel-like strength of his arms and chest seductive in their own right as I rested my head against his shoulder.

After a time, he settled me on my feet and stepped away, leaving me standing alone and unsure. I heard a door slide closed behind us, a lock click, and I hoped we were somewhere I would not have to hold back my cries of pleasure, for I knew they were to come. I had never done anything with a man before—I was completely untouched, but I knew he would pull them from me. I would give myself to him and he would give everything in return.

He let the tension build, made me wait and wonder

and worry. Anticipation built as I followed the sound of his feet as he paced in a circle around me.

I could feel his eyes on me once again. This time, I knew exactly how close he was. Hear the rustle of his clothing, breathe in his scent.

"Step out of your dress and kneel."

2

*H*elen

WE WERE INSIDE. I FELT SOFT CARPETING BENEATH MY knees as I lowered myself down to the floor, the air cooler than out in the garden and my nipples were hard points. I shivered, but it was from anticipation alone. My fingers obeyed before I had even registered his words.

My hands undid the clasp that held the garment on my shoulder, and I felt it slip down my body and pool at my feet. I took a small step forward, sliding the gown away with my other foot before dropping to my knees and placing my hands in my lap. I heard his breathing change, heard the pace of his footfalls slow as he continued his circle, no doubt studying my naked form.

"Unbind your hair."

Another order, but I complied at once, lifting my hands to my head and quickly unraveling the hard work of my new friends. When I was done, my hair floated around my shoulders. Kissing my skin, making me shiver once more.

"You are a virgin? Untouched?" he asked.

"Yes, Master."

No one had ever touched me, not like that. Men I'd dated before either didn't want me or didn't understand I needed to give over control, because none of them had ever made me feel like this. None of them had ever made my pussy this wet. This needy. Not one of them. I had no doubt he could see how wet I really was, how it slicked my thighs.

"Do you understand the Marked Mate Everian custom of the three sacred virginities?"

I nodded, thankful for the pseudo-orientation we'd received the day I'd arrived. "Yes."

On this planet, my mate would claim all three virginities. First my mouth, then my ass, and only when I fully accepted him as a mate for life, was he allowed to fuck me in the pussy. And plant his seed in my womb. I shuddered at the thought of him claiming me so thoroughly, of a baby being made, perhaps even that first time.

The Sacred Order of the three ensured he had to

seduce me first, gain my acceptance, before I would give him everything. Give him the sacred third virginity and claim him as my own forever. Like he said, he might be in control, but I held the power. I was the one to reject the claim, to decide to select another.

When I first heard of the custom, it had seemed odd. Strange. But then I realized it actually gave me more control over everything. There would be no true fucking, no children, no formal claiming until I gave him permission. To gain that permission, he had to woo me first. Had to make sure I wanted him. Wanted his touch, his kiss, his attention. While I was the one on my knees naked before him, I held all the control. I could say butterfly and this play between us would be over. I could say no and he wouldn't be able to claim me.

I was on my knees and yet he was at my mercy.

"Lift your hand." Doing as instructed, I lifted it into the air before me and his fingers wrapped around mine, pulling me gently to my feet.

He led me to a padded surface and instructed me to lie down on my back. With my hand in his, I lowered myself onto the cool leather that felt like a massage table back home.

"Good little mate," he murmured and I couldn't help but smile at the praise. His fingers squeezed mine, a hand on my hip to reassure me I was safe on the cushioned surface. He would not let me fall.

He took his time, restraining both my ankles and

my wrists, leaving me splayed and open before him. No, I definitely wasn't going to fall. A brief moment of panic hit me and I tugged at the bindings, but his words calmed me. "So beautiful, open for me like this. I can see all of you. Your lush curves." His finger slid over the outer swell of my full breast, then lower. "Soft skin." It moved around to my waist. "Gorgeous. Every inch of you."

I lifted my hips, wanting more of his light touch. Wanted him to move his fingers...*there.* But no. His fingertip was gone.

"I will touch all of you, lick, taste, suck, fuck. You're mine to do as I wish. What do you need to do to stop everything?"

Stop? I didn't want to stop. We were just getting started.

"Butterfly," I whispered, not wanting to say it too loudly, afraid he'd would truly halt his actions.

He squeezed my wrist gently. "Good little mate," he said again.

The words of praise filled me with satisfaction, and I couldn't help but smile.

I took a deep breath, let it out, gave a quick tug at the bindings once again. This was what I wanted. To be tied down and at his mercy. To know I could do nothing but submit. To give myself to him. The air suddenly felt cold on my open pussy as he walked around me once again, running his hand over my body, exploring everywhere, everywhere but *there*. He pushed my legs wide and the table moved beneath me on some sort of gear, spreading me open. He ran his huge hands up the inside of my thighs where I knew he could see how wet I was, feel it coating his palms, over my hipbones until he got a good grip and shifted me down toward him, toward the edge of the table. My bottom rested just at the hard edge and the motion bent my knees up so I was completely open. Completely vulnerable. Exposed. He could see me. All of me. There was no hiding.

"The first virginity to be taken is the mouth."

"But I thought—"

His hands slid down across my belly to my pussy and I gasped. My hips lifted involuntarily. His thumbs spread my slick lower lips wide. I didn't need my eyes to know exactly what he was looking at, and he was the first male to do so.

"Pink and wet. I can smell you. Sweet. I bet you taste that way. I'm going to find out. I can't wait a second longer to do so. When I'm done with you, don't worry, I'll claim that virgin mouth of yours and spill my seed down your throat. My balls ache with the need to do so, but I need your taste on my tongue first. Need to hear you scream your pleasure first."

He hadn't asked. He'd told me *exactly* what he was going to do. I could say my safe word, but when I felt his hot breath fan my sensitive folds, I bit my lip. And when his mouth clamped down on my clit, I bucked up off the table.

I bit my lip harder and when he lifted his head, I whimpered.

"Never stifle your pleasure, mate," he said, lifting his head. "I want to hear it all. Every pant, every moan. Every scream."

I could only nod, but when he didn't put his mouth back on me, I realized he was waiting for me. "Yes, Master. God, yes."

Seemingly satisfied, he worked me with his tongue, flicking the sensitive bud, first in circles, then on one side, then the other. He was seeing what I liked, how my body responded. And I responded, gasping and crying out, my muscles clenching and relaxing, toes curling. Sweat dampened my skin.

But all the attention to my clit made me realize the emptiness below. The rest of my pussy needed him and deep inside, I ached. I felt empty. I loved what he was doing, but I needed *more.*

Perhaps he was a mind reader or perhaps the Marked Mate bond was very strong, but he must have sensed my need and slid one finger inside me. Not too deep, and certainly cautious to prevent him from breaking through my hymen. If he was to claim my pussy last, I wanted his thick cock to truly breach me, not his blunt finger. I could only imagine what it would be like stretched open even wider by his cock. His finger was big enough. For now.

But when he stroked over a specific spot just inside my entrance, I moaned. There was no hiding the fact that I was practically dripping for him, the slick sound as loud as my ragged breathing. My legs began to shake. Quiver. When he flicked his tongue over one tiny spot of my clit, I screamed.

He worked my body like a master—my master—until I was thrashing against my restraints. Sweat slicked my skin. My breathing came in pants and I couldn't think of anything but him. I could do nothing but feel. To submit. I'd never been like this…on the precipice of something so intense, so powerful, I was afraid.

"Master, it's too much. I…oh, it's…help—"

"Let go, mate," he growled. "Give yourself to me. Do not fear it. There's nothing you can do but submit to the pleasure."

When I remembered he was right, that he controlled this, that I couldn't resist whatever he wanted to do to me, I let go. And when I did, the hot ball of pleasure exploded. My toes curled, my back arched. My scream bounced off the walls of the room. I was falling and floating, yet anchored to the table. I'd made myself come before, but it had been nothing like this. Not body consuming, intense pleasure. My pussy clenched rhythmically around his finger and spasmed. I felt my body get wetter, dripping from me to coat his hand. I wanted more, needed him deeper. My pussy was ready, wet, slick and eager for him.

The sensations lessened, yet he didn't let up. In fact, he sucked harder, making me cry out once again. It was too much. I was too sensitive, the feelings too intense. I didn't understand them, couldn't control them. I was overwhelmed and I tried to jerk away, my head thrashed on the padded surface. I tried to close my legs and the restraints dug into my flesh reminding me that I could not move. I was open and at his complete mercy. If he wanted me to feel more, then I would. I had no choice. The knowledge sent me into another orgasm as he continued to fuck me with his curling finger and the flicks of his tongue.

Tears slipped down my temples, my hair clung to my cheeks. My legs quivered and my heels pressed into the padded top.

"It's too much," I pleaded. "I can't..."

While his finger stilled inside me, he lifted his head to speak. "Do you wish to say the one word that will stop everything?"

Did I? Did I want him to stop? To end his attentions? Did I want to be the one who said enough when we were just getting started or would I trust in him to know what was best for me? Even if it was pleasure almost beyond bearing?

I licked my dry lips. "No, Master."

His free hand slid up and down the inside of my thigh in a reassuring gesture. "Such a good little mate. I know what you need. You're dripping your cream all over my palm, my mouth. It's on my chin."

His tongue flicked out, brushed over my clit. So gently, like the wings of the butterfly I wanted to be.

"So sensitive. So perfect. Your taste. Sweet and ripe. And all for me." He lapped at me. "Every drop."

I came again, but this time, there was no scream. It was caught in my throat. The pleasure was rolling, a gentle, deep wave that swamped me. Took me under.

As I began to return to myself—how long had the pleasure lasted I had no idea— he moved, kissing his way down my leg and up the other side to my hip, across my stomach until he reached my breasts where he took his time sucking first one nipple, then the other into his mouth. I felt his body pressing into my open pussy, the rough brush of his pants against my tender, sensitive skin. I could feel the bulge of his cock, but he did nothing with it. Only that thin layer of his clothing kept him from sinking into me. I clenched my inner walls with the need to be filled by such girth.

Only his mouth worked me. He kissed every inch of me. Until he reached my mouth and his kiss stole my breath. It was our first kiss, his lips firm and insistent. Gentle and persuasive. The taste of my passion still on his tongue was new and exciting and strange. Intimate.

"See how sweet you taste?" he murmured against my lips.

He moved then, walking around the table to stand by my head.

He adjusted the table again, cupping my arms and moving me once more, this time carefully sliding me toward him, toward the top of the table so my legs were straight and he carefully settled my head so it hung over the edge. My neck arched back as I heard the rustle of clothing.

Oh my. When the officiate mentioned the claiming of the first virginity, I'd imagined me on my knees, cock in hand as I laved and sucked him with my mouth. Not like this. Never had I even imagined doing it like this.

I might be a virgin, but I knew what was coming, knew that soon his cock would fill my mouth. I was eager for a taste of it, to feel it against my tongue, to have my lips stretched wide. Eager to be his in this first official claiming.

"Open your mouth, mate," he ordered. "Open up and suck this cock deep."

I did as ordered and immediately the thick head of him was on my tongue, my lips stretched wide. He was huge, so big I wasn't sure I could take all of him. But he leaned over me somehow until I felt smothered by his presence. Buried under him as if he were a blanket. He slowly pushed his cock deep, then retreated, allowing me time to work it with my tongue, to get him all wet and slick before he pushed deeper into my throat. As I gasped at the intrusion, two of his fingers dipped into my pussy. My groan vibrated through his shaft.

Two fingers. Oh my god. So big he was stretching me open. Mouth and pussy.

He held still for long seconds, the flared tip nudging into my throat as my tongue licked along the shaft. I thought perhaps I would have to tap the table to ask for air, but he pulled back and I gasped for breath. As his fingers fucked me harder, demanding another orgasm from my overwrought body, he plunged in and out of my mouth. *This* was fucking. A little rough, and yet I knew he was still holding back.

"Your mouth is too hot. Wet. Your throat constricts around me." His voice was a rough growl. If his cock wasn't down my throat, I'd think he were mad. No, he was at the end of his control. In that moment, I felt powerful. "Fuck, I won't last."

His flavor was wild and exotic, nothing I'd ever tasted before. I craved it, wanted more as he didn't relent. Wet sounds mixed with his ragged breathing. I was determined to make him come, to make him lose control and pump his seed down my throat.

Hollowing my cheeks, I sucked him hard, to pull him into me, determined to claim him, leave my mark not just on his body, but his soul. I was a virgin in this, but with him, I felt skilled. Felt like I could make *him* lose control.

Perhaps I shocked him with my vigor because he groaned and then shouted my name as his hot cum pulsed in thick streams down my throat. I swallowed, sucked harder, then swallowed some more, single-minded in my need to draw it from him, forcing him to give it to me even as his brash order registered. There was so much, as if he'd been storing it up just to fill me with it.

"Come now."

And just like that, with those two words uttered on a dark snarl, I shattered again. Too weak to resist. Unable to do anything but give him what he wanted. My body was eager to respond to the slightest command, my body rhythmically clenching his fingers trying to pull them in even deeper. A few orgasms and I was trained to do his bidding.

He pulled his cock from my mouth and shifted me again so my head was flat once more on the table. A finger swiped a drop of seed from the corner of my mouth as I caught my breath.

I could hear his ragged inhales, knew he was taking a moment as well.

The restraints were removed, but I remained still as his hands gently massaged my body until I was a limp, sweaty pool. I had to wonder if my bones had dissolved. My thighs were wet from my arousal, my skin sticky. The salty taste of his cum coated my tongue, the quantity of it filling my belly. He kissed me over and over and worshipped every inch of my skin as if he would never get enough before helping me to sit up. I sat placidly as he lowered the dress over my head, adjusted it and I felt his fingers as he fastened the clasp at my shoulder.

From one heartbeat to the next, I was back in his arms and carried outside, the humid air caressing my heated skin. He lowered me to the familiar hard feel of the stone bench. He placed a kiss right below my ear as he leaned down and whispered, "You were perfect, mate. I am so proud of you. Of how you responded to my touch, how you took my cock so beautifully. I will come to you in your rooms at the same time tomorrow night for more. My cock is eager once again for you, as am I. Be dressed in black and blindfolded as you are now."

His deep voice caressed every inch of my body and I leaned into his touch, not ready to be parted from him. I wanted to stay in his arms forever. But that was not to be. He was silent and waited.

"Yes, Master," I breathed.

And then he was gone. I knew he had left, felt it. Knew I was once again alone. Only the aching pleasure in my pussy and a swollen, sensitive clit lingered like the sweetest drug in my system. The taste of him in my mouth, the tightness in my jaw proved the first claiming was over. He was everything I'd imagined and yet I had nothing real. Not even his name.

H unter Zee, the Touchstone

HOLY FUCK. SHE WAS PERFECT. HER LONG BROWN HAIR hung in waves spun with random pieces of red and gold. Her lips were plump and ripe and her mouth so hot and wet and…eager. My cock pulsed remembering just how much. She'd conquered me as easily as if I were a young man new to the pleasures of my cock. Her body was perfect; soft skin, generous curves. Everything about her was perfect. Passionate. Obedient. Submissive. Beautiful.

But I was not.

My Marked Mate, Helen from Earth, was everything I'd imagined but never expected to have. I knew from watching her from across the room that her laughter came easily and her eyes were a unique combination of green and gold I'd never seen before. I longed to have her look at me and know me. Know exactly who claimed her. Who mastered her body. Whose soul she'd invaded with more ruthlessness and cunning than the Hive a battlegroup quadrant.

I longed to have those eyes focused on me not just in pleasure, but with love. Affection. Desire. With the soft gaze of a submissive eager to please. But those were a fool's dreams. Those thoughts did not belong to a scarred warrior like me.

Perhaps if I could seduce her, bring her enough pleasure, she would learn to tolerate my appearance. It was the best I could hope for, but that hope burned and twisted inside me like hot knives. Wanting her was painful, but it was an agony I refused to give up. I knew the sight of her body, the feel of her pussy, the taste of it, the tightness of her throat as she swallowed me down.

I strode to my quarters, my balls empty, my body sated by the pleasure of my one perfect female. Gods, I'd claimed her first virginity. She'd allowed it. Given it to me. Enjoyed it. Even came from the pleasure of it. Of submitting to me. Of course, I'd ensured her desire and completion...several times first, but she'd been right there with me. I'd hovered over her pussy, wanted to feel her clench down on my fingers just as her cheeks pulled taut around my cock.

Me.

My cock. My seed filled her belly. My mouth and fingers had brought her pleasure. Made her writhe and scream. Beg and pant.

As I nodded to a group of Hunters who passed on the garden path, I had to wonder if one of them would be better suited. None of them would need to blindfold their Marked Mate to fuck her. While I'd brought her to climax several times, she hadn't known who had done it. She didn't know my face, my name. All she knew was the blunt head of my cock, the thick girth of it, the taste of my cum as it splashed down her throat.

None of the other Hunters would be terrified, as I was, that the very sight of them would cause a beautiful young innocent to run away in fear. It happened often enough, the sight of my scars making females run away in horror. Helen didn't know about the Hive, the damage and destruction they caused, but looking at me, she'd know first-hand. I would not be the sight that made her afraid of not only her mate, but what was out there.

But even the thought of my mate with another brought my hunting instincts to the fore and I had to fight to control the urge to attack the Hunters as they passed. Instead, I focused on the lingering taste of Helen's sweet pussy on my tongue, the sound of her cries as she'd come apart for me, giving me everything. Again and again.

Helen had submitted. Beautifully. Following my every command, giving over her control in mind and body. To her Marked Mate. She'd wanted it, saw the evidence of her need, tasted it.

The burning of my palm and my sated cock were proof she was mine.

But she wasn't. Not yet, even with one virginity claimed. Perhaps not ever. Not truly.

She accepted me, for now. At least, I could pretend she was mine as long as she didn't see me. I could hold out hope.

A group of brides walked by. After getting a good look at my face, their expressions changed from carefree laughter to horror. As usual. Their pace quickened and their whispers lingered long after they did.

I was used to it. I was scary looking. Dangerous in appearance. Ruthless. It mattered not how I'd come by the injuries. It mattered not that, among other fighters, the scars were proof of bravery, of service. But with the females, with my mate? It wasn't a badge of honor but a mottling of skin that caused revulsion and disgust.

Gods. I even scared new Hunters—perhaps because I was a reminder of what had happened to me could easily happen to them when battling the Hive. And now, retired from service, I wondered why I was assigned to the Touchstone, where innocent and naïve virgins were brought to find their mates. It was beyond me.

But here I was, the feared one. Not that I would

shirk my duties. No, these females were all safe on my watch. No harm would befall them.

I hadn't always been this way. *Damaged.* No. One battle and I was ruined. Injured by an ion blast and pinned behind enemy lines. I'd escaped the Hive, but I'd been on the run for days and the wounds to my body had healed before I could reach a ReGen pod. There was nothing the doctors could do. I was scarred for life. Ruthless slices and mottled skin marred my face, my neck. To a female, I was hideous. The virgin brides who'd walked by were proof of that.

And yet I'd been blessed by the gods to find my Marked Mate. Other Hunters were envious of me—for that alone. My mark had guided me to her and the dreams we shared proved the bond. The way she submitted and came for me as well. But she would not want me if she saw me, saw the disfigurement. She would be horrified. Afraid. Scared of me. The one word I feared she'd utter, *butterfly*, would come from her lush lips and it wouldn't be from pushing her too far sexually. It would be from a quick glance alone.

I couldn't survive her rejection. Everyone else in the universe I could handle. But sweet, innocent, pure Helen? Seeing fear or loathing in her eyes would destroy what was left of me. I'd thought myself invulnerable after the ion blast attack. Nothing else could hurt me. Nothing in the war or on my home world would ever be able to bring me low. I was a survivor. Strong. So much stronger than the others.

Yet one touch and Helen made me weak. The flare of my mark made me vulnerable. The taste of her on my tongue made me powerless.

"Well?" Hunter Quinn asked, slapping me on the back as I came through the grand entry of the building. We were cousins, of a size, yet where I was dark he was golden light with chiseled features and an unmarred form. The women of Everis frequently offered themselves to him, yet he waited for a Marked Mate. He was an eternal optimist, full of patience for what I had received.

A fool whose grin was broader than mine.

"She's perfect," I admitted, thinking of her sitting on the garden bench waiting for me. Her dark hair, soft curves, gentle smile. Then on her knees naked. On the table spread wide and at my mercy. Of her mouth, stretched wide around my cock.

"I told you." Quinn was not yet mated. We'd fought together for years and had been stationed at the Touchstone for the past six months. He was hopeful of a match of his own. Eager for it. And when my mark flared to life only a few nights ago, when I'd woken up exhausted from dream sharing and with my cock hard as a rock, he'd been jealous. Happy for me.

Gods, too fucking happy for me. He just didn't understand.

"What's the matter?" he asked. "Your cock flagged too soon?"

His sly grin backed his jest.

"Asshole," I growled. "Her first virginity is claimed."

He slapped me on the back again. We moved away from the doorway as other Hunters wanted entry.

"Then what's the matter?" He grabbed my arm, tugged me to a corner. When I didn't respond, he continued, looking around. "Fuck, Zee, where is she? Why isn't she with you?"

I put my hands on my hips. "She's not with me because I refuse to let her see me."

His expression went flat. "What?"

I sighed, looked away. "If she sees me, she won't want me."

He frowned. "So how the hell did you fuck her mouth?"

"Blindfold."

"Blindfold?"

"She's submissive. Wants me to take control. It's… incredible." That wasn't a strong enough word, but I couldn't think of one better. Not now in my post-orgasm haze.

The corner of his mouth quirked up, but he remained silent. Waited.

"I blindfolded her to enhance the experience."

"Bullshit," he countered. "You blindfolded her so she wouldn't see your scars. How many fucking times have I told you your Marked Mate—if you were lucky enough to have your mark awakened—won't give a shit what you look like? The match has been made since birth. It won't change because of a few scars."

I shook my head, knowing the truth. He'd said the same to me again and again, but it mattered not.

I knew. Helen wouldn't want me if she saw me.

And then I'd be alone.

————

HELEN

THE OTHER NEW BRIDE ARRIVALS GATHERED AROUND THE breakfast table laughing and giggling, their eyes full of hope and excitement. As women do, a few shared details of their first night with their new mates, Hunters eager to stake their claims and make themselves known. Some had found their Marked Mates—only a few, including me—the rest having found a male who they clicked with. It seemed one didn't have to be marked to have an instant connection. The males they spoke of were proud of their new mates, of the claiming process they were now in.

Not mine. My Marked Mate kept me in the dark— literally—and while I loved everything that had happened between us, I felt vulnerable. Unsure. Why had he refused to reveal himself to me? Was he undecided about me? The mark on my palm was hot and pulsing, even now, but was that a guarantee? Was he not pleased or proud of me?

While he'd come down my throat, I knew it to be an

automatic response in men. I'd gotten him off, but had I not pleased him?

He'd come to me last night in my dreams, but had done nothing but hold me as if I were the most precious thing in the world. Breakable china. He'd insisted I keep my eyes closed, and I'd been happy to obey, listening to the strong beat of his heart and melting into his heat as his hands stroked my back.

I'd never felt safer, or more loved. But he hadn't dominated, hadn't pinned me to the bed and taken what he wanted. He hadn't ravaged me. He'd kept the passion at bay.

Even with that I could be okay. But why did he deny me the one thing I needed? Why wouldn't he reveal himself?

What if he didn't want a mate? He'd said nothing about a future together. Nothing about claiming me, keeping me, making me his forever. Had I come across the galaxy for a fling? Because I could have had that back home on Earth a hundred times over.

Sure, he'd talked about the three sacred virginities, but still. Was I just a faceless woman to him? It was said the eyes were the gateway to the soul. Was he covering mine to keep himself distant?

I sighed. So many questions and I had no answers.

I'd hoped he'd reveal more than his face to me. I wanted him to *give* himself to me.

"You're too quiet, Helen. What's up? Are you all right?" Lexi spoke from her seat on my left. Lexi was gorgeous, with long black hair and dark eyes. I knew she'd met her mate, a Hunter named Von, and judging by the flushed look on her cheeks and the happy glow in her eyes, she wasn't grappling with the same doubts I had this morning. Had I looked like that after my mate had made me come? I hadn't been able to help the smile that had formed on my lips after he'd given me the best orgasm of my life.

"I'm fine."

"Liar." She took a sip of her juice and leaned in close. "Spill. Maybe we can help." By *we*, she referred to her two best friends, Dani and Katie. Of the three, Lexi was the only one who smiled like everything was right in the universe. Katie scowled, as if angry every time the Hunter named Bryn walked by. And Dani, poor Dani looked even more miserable than I felt.

They'd transported just the other day from Earth as well and had formed a quick, tight bond. While I wasn't as close with them, they were friendly. Kind. And now, the three of them looked at me with concern.

"I don't think you can help me," I said, flicking my gaze to my lap.

"Try us." Katie lifted a dark brown brow over blue eyes, managing to look both regal and annoyed all at the same time. The look made me grin.

I sighed once again. "All right."

They leaned in close and I felt like I was whispering secrets in seventh grade math class.

"I met my Marked Mate."

"Yes!" Lexi pumped her fist as Dani tilted her head and Katie raised both brows.

"So what's the problem?" Katie asked.

"I don't know who he is," I admitted. I glanced about, thinking maybe he was here…somewhere. But no. He'd only make his appearance later when I was waiting, blindfold once again in place.

"What do you mean you don't know who he is? Have you met him? Has he—you know—claimed your first virginity?" Lexi blushed, but she didn't mince words. I could tell by the way she waggled her eyebrows she knew more about it than just what the officiate had told us during orientation. She, no doubt, had had her mate's cock in her mouth very recently.

"Yes. But he made me wear a blindfold and won't tell me his name." I tried not to pout but it was pretty hard.

"What about your dreams? You do dream share like they say, right?" Dani's arms were crossed, her elbows resting on the edge of the table. She was petite and blonde, like a prima ballerina. Tiny and perfect. The way she tilted her head, the way she kept her voice soft and even made me want to tell her everything. While she was happy for me, she seemed to have less… eagerness about the whole Marked Mate thing than Katie.

I nodded. "He makes me keep my eyes closed in our dreams, too."

39

"That *is* weird," Katie blurted, then bit her lip when she realized how loud she'd spoken.

Dani slapped her on the arm. "That's not helpful."

Lexi was staring at the mark on her palm as if the stupid thing would give her answers. I waited. Maybe it would. Maybe she would come up with some genius suggestion, because I had no idea what to do. She took a deep breath and lifted her dark gaze to mine. "Do you want him? Is he *The One*?"

I thought of his deep voice, his gentle hands, the way his commands made my body melt and sing at the same time. What he'd done with his mouth and fingers. "Yes. I want him." *God, yes.*

Lexi and Dani leaned in even closer and I did the same as Lexi asked her next question. "When are you seeing him again? In person, I mean."

"Tonight, in my rooms."

Her eyes sparkled with mischief and I knew, whatever she suggested, I was going to do it. "Does he want you to wear a blindfold again?"

"Yes."

"Then just don't." She offered a simple shrug with those words. As if it were just that easy.

I shook my head. "No. I can't do that. I have to...I mean, I *want* to follow his commands." I blushed admitting that, but none of the girls gave me grief.

"They are dominant, these Hunters, aren't they?" Lexi asked, that wide grin showing she liked it when her mate took charge, too. "I see the way you're blushing. Don't worry, I like it the way Von's all bossy and gruff. And when he's doing things to me…" She looked off dreamily for a second, then caught herself. Eyed Katie and Dani, then let her smile slip. "If you have to wear a blindfold, then you'll borrow it from me."

I glanced at Katie, whose mouth formed an *Oh* before stretching into a wide grin. "Oooh, you are evil."

"Evil? I don't understand," I replied, frowning. And I didn't. I had no idea what the heck was going on. What were they planning?

Lexi rubbed her palms together with glee. "You'll have to dim the lights a little, so he can't see the material very well."

"What are you talking about?"

Her smile made me want to smile back, so I did. Her eagerness was infectious and my curiosity was definitely piqued.

"I have some material you can use to make a blindfold. It's see-through, you know. So you can obey his command and see him at the same time."

"And if you keep the lights dim like Lexi suggested, he'll never know you cheated," Katie added. "Just keep your eyes closed until you're pretty sure he's not looking at your—umm—face."

"Yeah, your curves are enough to make a grown man fall to his knees," Dani added, checking out my chest, cupping her hands in front of her chest. I glanced down. Compared to hers, I had cantaloupes for boobs. "If you've got them, use them to your advantage."

When Lexi and Katie just stared at her wide-eyed, Dani burst out laughing. "What?" she shrugged. "Just saying."

I sipped my juice, sure my face was as red as the strange fruit in the bowl in front of us. I debated their plan, wondering if it was a good idea. If I did what Lexi suggested, I'd be able to see him, study him. But what if I got caught? Would he not want me anymore? He'd definitely be mad. And he'd definitely spank me. He'd mentioned that would happen if I didn't obey. The idea of being spanked wasn't that appealing, but when *he'd* talked about it, it had only made me hot. And wet. Was I willing to face the consequences if I were caught? Hell, yes. I squirmed in my chair, but I wasn't sure if it was from a potential punishment or because my pussy ached with need for more of only what my mate could give me.

But when breakfast was over, I didn't resist as Lexi led me to her room. In fact, I was more eager than ever.

4

H elen

DINNER HAD COME AND GONE AND THE HOUR GREW LATE as I waited. I sat on the corner of my bed, my back straight and chin held high as I anticipated my mate's arrival. The gown I wore was black silk—just as he'd requested—but it clung to every curve with a gentleness that made my skin sensitive. It hung to the floor, covering the black thigh-high stockings and garters I'd asked Lexi to help me get this morning. I added a barely there G-string and no bra to complete the indecent outfit. On the outside, the off-the-shoulder gown made me look regal and composed.

Underneath, I was dressed for pure sin.

He'd wanted me to wear black, but hadn't given

more specific details. And so the four of us—me, along with Lexi, Katie and Dani—had filled those details in for ourselves. Sexy details that would make a male pant and, hopefully, lose control.

This sooo wasn't me, but desperate times called for desperate measures. Meaning, a sexy outfit. Even a touch slutty. I *had* taken him deep in my throat, so I did have a little bit of an inner slut. I grinned to myself.

Dani had helped me with my makeup, and my lips were bright red and glossy, my skin flawless. I knew my mate couldn't see my eyes, but they were shadowed to perfection just in case he decided to look.

I wanted him to look. I wanted him to rip the blindfold off and look me in the eyes, declare his love for me. Tell me he wanted me forever and beg me to allow him to claim my pussy as his own.

But that was a dream. Tonight, I had one goal. One.

To see him. To learn his identity. I needed to know what he was hiding. No—*why* he was hiding from me.

The pearlescent blindfold that covered my eyes was pure genius. The outer appearance was reflective ivory, but from the inside I could see through it as if I were looking through a two-way mirror. I could look at him, watch him, *see him*. And as long as I stayed out of direct light, he'd have no idea I was disobeying him in this small way. I'd tested it with the ladies, making sure the lighting was right, that I could see them, but confirmed they couldn't tell.

Disobeying? Definitely, but I considered it more bending his request to fit my needs, too.

As the door to my chamber slid open, I was careful to tilt my head as if I could hear him, not see the giant shadow of a man lurking in the doorway. Not just any man. *Him.* My mate. My mysterious, secretive mate. My heart pounded as he approached, but I held myself still. Waiting.

I needed to obey him—at least in everything but the blindfold. I needed him to be happy. The war within me was real, and almost painful at the thought that I was deceiving him. That I might disappoint him.

But I remained silent. I had to know.

The quiet of the room stretched and he took two steps closer, his face hidden in shadow as the door slid closed behind him. I had the room lighted by a handful of scented candles I'd asked Officiate Treva to help me find. She'd scowled, informed me that open flames were forbidden in the Touchstone, then winked and taken me to one of a handful of S-Gen units, Spontaneous Matter Generators, and asked me what scent I wanted.

It had been like watching a scene from *Star Trek* as she'd talked to the machine and five ivory candles had appeared, scented with cinnamon and vanilla.

Now those candles flickered and glowed in the darkness of my bedroom as my mate approached.

My hair was up in a twist, baring my neck and shoulders and I held my breath as his fingers trailed over my collarbones, my jaw. His touch was soft. Reverent.

"You are very beautiful, Helen."

The sound of his voice sank deep into my bones, the words warming me as much as the feel of his skin on mine.

"Do you know what happens tonight?" he asked.

I gave a small nod, but kept my head angled down. Just the feel of his caress had my nipples pebbling and I wanted more. I wanted what we'd shared the night before, and more. Yet I was afraid for him to learn of my duplicity and be angry. If he were to do that, to punish me for my disobedience, I wanted it to be later. But I would see him first. And have him claim my second virginity.

For if he did, I would be one step closer to being his.

And he one step closer to being mine.

Tied to me irrevocably just as much as I would be his. Permanently.

"Yes, Master."

"Say it."

I licked my suddenly dry lips. "You'll claim me again."

"Yes, but where?"

Gods, it was a little embarrassing. I hadn't even considered this type of sex until coming here, until Officiate Treva mentioned it. Oh, I knew what it was, of course, but had never considered doing it myself. And now, with him, I wanted it. I clenched my pussy and ass at the very thought. After the way he'd brought me pleasure the day before, I knew he'd make this good, too. I had no fears.

I would give myself to him in this as well.

And so I took a deep breath and told him. "You'll claim my ass."

"My good little mate."

When he took my chin and tipped it up, I kept my eyes closed. I wasn't ready yet. But when his lips met mine, when his tongue delved deep to find mine, to play, I forgot all about seeing him. I *felt.*

And when he lifted his head and traced the edges of my gown with his fingertips, I dared. My eyes fluttered open, I saw him for the first time. *Him.*

Big. Broad. Dark hair, strong brow, square jaw. Blunt nose. Full lips. Eyes that held fierce need. Heat. Love.

I saw all of that in a blink of an eye, for while I'd never seen him before, had no idea to his appearance, I *knew* him. Deep down. My mark pulsed. Throbbed along with my pussy.

And then I saw what he'd been trying to hide. Not at first, mind you, but seconds later. Scars. All over his face, his neck. One sliced through his eyebrow and down his cheek.

He was marred by what I assumed was battle. His kisses lingered, tracing the line of my jaw, my cheek. I lifted my hands to him, eager to touch and explore, to claim what was mine.

The moment my hand settled over the scars on his neck, he reached for me, pulled my hands from him. He was breathing heavily, panting as if he'd just run a marathon, as he lowered my hands and held them in front of me. He locked my wrists in a gentle grip where I could not touch him, could not learn the truth with my fingertips. Restrained but without any bindings.

But it was too late. I knew him. Knew his face. Knew he was mine. Yes, he was the one for me. Scars and all.

"Mate," he breathed.

It broke me from my staring, and I tilted my head down again. My heart pounded in my ears, afraid he'd seen my eyes, saw me staring. Knew I *knew* the truth. Would he yell, rile, punish?

I'd heard his name was Zee, the Hunter with the scars. He was infamous here at the Touchstone. He was frightening to the other brides, a monster among gods when he walked with the other Hunters. I'd heard much speculation about how he'd gotten his scars, but no one dared to ask. With the advanced technology of the alien races, it had to have been something terrible. Too horrible to imagine.

The thought made my heart ache for him, and I had to clench my jaw and bite my tongue to hold back words of sorrow or sympathy. Something. The pain he'd had suffered through must have been horrible. Everything was churning inside me until I couldn't sort through the emotions.

He was hiding his scars. I wanted to reach up, touch them, feel every rough line, every white stripe that burdened him. Kiss each one. The weight of them was heavy upon his shoulders, upon his heart if he would not share them with me. Me! His Marked Mate.

His soul must be as battered and torn as his face.

"Mate, the kiss was not enough," he murmured, his voice an octave lower. "We've only just begun this night."

I shivered at the possibility, yet my mind was awash in his pain. In his need to hide. He gave to me so thoroughly, learning my body and giving it the pleasure I didn't even know I craved. He cared for me, I sensed it. Somehow, perhaps, even protecting me from himself? What was I to do? I couldn't pull down the blindfold. I couldn't let on that I knew. I sensed…no, I knew, he was a proud male. I could not harm him further by letting on that I knew. But there was one thing he could share—

"May I ask one question, Master?"

"What is it, my little mate?"

"While I will still call you Master, please tell me your name."

He was quiet. Still. I *felt* his stillness. Had I overstepped? Had he figured out I'd seen him?

"To you, and you alone, my name is Master. Your Master." His voice was hard, filled with rough command that made my pussy clench and my mind whirl at the same time. He wasn't ready to tell me and I had to accept that. Was he, too, aware of his infamy at the Touchstone? Was he worried if I knew his name that I'd know the truth? Maybe, if I could convince him that I was totally and completely his, he would feel safe enough to share everything with me. His trust would be all the more precious once I'd earned it, so I did not push.

"Thank you, Master."

"Now, mate." He took my hand, held it. "Stand. My fingers itch to remove your dress."

I stood then with his help and kept my eyes downcast as his hands undid the fastenings of my dress and let it fall to the floor.

"Mate," he said. The word was drawn out on a groan as I stood before him. I knew what he was seeing.

"Yes, Master?" I squeaked.

"Your command was to dress in black and be blindfolded. I did not request…this."

Through the blindfold, I could see his arms lift, as if indicating what still covered my body. He didn't like the stockings, the scrap of panties?

"I'm sorry I—"

He cut me off. "I should punish you for disobeying, but I can't deny something so lovely. So fucking hot."

His fingers took hold of one of my garters, plucked it like a rubber band. The slight sting of satin against my thigh had me gasp, my nipples tighten further. Oh god. I'd wanted him to be all hot and bothered and now I was, too.

"My balls are heavy with cum for you. And this sight? My virgin is also a vixen."

I couldn't help the small smile that played on my lips. He liked it. No, he loved what I wore. With my eyes angled down, I could see the thick bulge of his cock beneath his uniform pants.

I felt, all at once, wickedly powerful. While he gave all the orders, I was truly in control. I could say my safe word, but there was no need.

He wanted me as much as I desired him. Perhaps this need would be what would eventually win him over, to prove to him, somehow, that this was more. This was forever and I wanted all of him.

If I were going to give him all of me, then it had to be even.

But now? With him all but salivating over me, it wasn't the time to press the issue.

I'd forget about seeing more of him and just submit. I'd give myself to him tonight. Tomorrow? Tomorrow, I wanted forever. I wanted his name. He would give me his name before he claimed my pussy. He would give me a gift and I would figure out how to give him everything in return.

"Claiming your ass is to be taken slowly. To prepare you for my cock takes time." He took a deep breath. "But vixen, I believe you are as eager as me. Ripe. Wet."

"Yes, Master," I readily admitted. I was wet. The

scrap of my G-string was ruined and did nothing to hide my needy state. My pussy ached to be filled, but I knew I was to be denied. Perhaps that was why I was eager for his cock. In my ass.

"But first I need more of your taste." He tipped my chin up and kissed me again, his hands cupping the sides of my face tilting and turning me exactly the way he wanted. The kiss was tender and fierce, dominant and potent. Everything I ever imagined. Intimate, too. He wasn't just bringing me pleasure, we were connecting. I felt his need for that bond in his lips, his tongue, the gentle pressure of his fingers. In every hard line of his body as he pressed against me. Clothed to barely clothed.

He broke the kiss after I don't know how long with a sigh, a brush of our noses. In that instant, he was tender. A different kind of lover. Not one who intended to fill my ass with his big cock and empty his cum there, marking me as deep as possible. Then he nibbled along my jaw, down my neck, licked along my collarbone, then dropped to his knees.

I remained still as he kissed my breasts, then took one nipple into his mouth and suckled. Okay, *there* was the passionate lover.

My hands went to his shoulders of their own volition. Realizing I perhaps shouldn't have done that, I dropped them.

"No. You may touch me," he breathed, his breath

fanning over my wet nipple, making it furl even tighter.

I put my hands back on his hard, broad shoulders and felt the play of his muscles beneath my fingertips. The heat from him radiated through his shirt. It felt good to hold on, especially since he returned to play with my breasts.

He didn't linger there—I had no idea they were so sensitive—only built up my need for him to a fever, then kissed down my belly. I shifted my hands to his hair when he curled his fingers into the thin strings of my G-string and tugged, pulling it down to the floor before licking over my pussy.

I cried out, gripped the thick, silky locks, held on tight. It wasn't overlong, but enough to hold on to. To keep his face right between my thighs and so I wouldn't fall. Or float away. Or have him stop.

When he flicked my clit so expertly, I went up on my toes, almost too much pleasure with that one lick.

"You will take the pleasure I give, little mate."

Taking a deep breath, letting it out, I relaxed. And then he took me to the brink and over with just his tongue, his hands cupping my bottom and holding me up.

When my legs were wobbly, only then did he let me come. I cried out my pleasure, rocking and shifting my hips almost riding his face. I didn't want the bliss to end. Ever.

But he tempered his caress and my body softened, became very sated.

He said, "Turn around and lean over the bed."

I glanced down at him, saw him wipe his glistening mouth with the back of his hand. Yes, I was wet. So wet I could feel it slick on my thighs. I didn't stare for long, remembering myself—even in my post-orgasm haze— and did as he said, spinning on my heel and bending at the waist, putting my hands on the soft blanket. I faced away from him, in the perfect position for him to spank me if he learned the truth. I bit my lip, dipped my head so my forehead touched the soft blanket.

"Stick that ass out," he commanded. "Show me everything."

Shifting my feet, I curled my back, thrust my butt out and back. I could only imagine what I looked like. Bent over the bed. Naked besides stockings and garters. My breasts swayed from the shift in position, my hair fell in soft tendrils now over my neck. If Lexi thought I looked sexy all put together, surely it was nothing compared to this. I felt like I was in a porn flick, especially with the blindfold on.

He'd prepared me so well, taking what he had the night before, something familiar, to ease me into this next step. I was ready. I was eager. My pussy was desperate, although that wasn't what he'd claim next. So was I. The idea of him taking my ass was no longer scary. I wanted it. I wanted him. In me, any way I could get him. I was hot for him. Frantic. Desperate. The orgasm that still sizzled over every one of my nerve endings only made me needier.

I wanted more…*him.*

A palm slid over my upturned bottom. "Gorgeous. It will look even better pink with my handprints."

I startled. Had he learned the truth? "You'll…you'll spank me?" I asked, staring down at the bed, clenching every muscle, holding my breath. Waiting for that palm to land.

"For punishment, if needed. For pleasure, definitely. Not tonight. Soon."

I sighed, relaxed. For some strange reason, I was slightly disappointed.

My hips wiggled involuntarily at the thought and I heard his chuckle. "I see you like the idea." He gave me a light swat and I gasped. It wasn't hard and it didn't hurt, but I now understood what he meant by for pleasure. The slight sting morphed into heat and spread throughout my body. Made my pussy gush with my arousal, my clit swell and pulse with the need for more.

"I can see your eagerness from here. Smell it. Fuck, mate. You are my undoing."

When I felt his fingers slide over my pussy, I gasped. He groaned.

"Dripping."

I should have been mortified at my response, but I wasn't. I was wet and eager, ready for my Marked Mate to fuck me. It was the ultimate symbol of my need for him. I could lie with words and tell him otherwise, but my body boldly displayed the truth. I was his and my pussy was stating I belonged to him.

My pussy belonged to him. And when he slid one of those drenched fingers up to my back hole and circled it, I knew this taboo spot would soon be his as well. I gasped at the illicit contact, cried out as he pressed inward. Groaned when I began to open for him.

I wiggled my hips again and he slipped inside.

"Oh, god," I moaned, when a finger breached me there. It was an odd feeling, opening for him. Remaining that way. I couldn't help but clench, to try and push him out, but like everything else he did, he would not be dissuaded. He ruled my body. It felt tight, strangely deep even though it had to be just a fingertip. And big. I'd only seen the outline of his cock through the sheer blindfold, but I'd also had it in my mouth… down my throat. I knew it was much bigger than this, that I'd be stretched open and then even more before the second claiming was done.

He retreated and I let out a breath I hadn't realized I was holding.

"No rush, little mate. I'll take all the time you need to be ready. We'll get this tight little hole all slick and open for me."

I felt the cold drizzle of what I assumed was lube down the seam of my bottom. Where had that come from? Pocket? He hadn't moved from my side so it couldn't have been tucked in a drawer or something so—

"Oh, my god," I said again, my random wonderings forgotten because this time, when he slipped a finger in, he reached beneath me and stroked my clit at the same time. Sensitive from the orgasm and the workings of his tongue, I responded instantly. And, wow, it was different. Nerve endings I didn't know I had came to life. Sizzled. The combination of ass play and clit attention was lethal to my control.

When he carefully fucked my ass with just the tip of his finger, slowly in and out, I came. I screamed, the intensity of it had my arms collapsing. I fell onto my forearms, which made his finger pop out.

I tingled there, clenched, wishing he was back inside. Sweat bloomed on my skin, and I couldn't catch my breath. I wanted more. That had been wicked bliss. Intense, powerful and…wow.

He leaned over me, his chest pressed to my back. But there was no shirt, only bare, hot skin. He'd stripped and I felt the hot press of his cock against my pussy, felt it slip through my juices, the slick lube. Thick. Long. Hot. And it was all for me. And it was all going *in* me.

"I knew you'd like it," he breathed. He was so calm, so focused on me, but his cock was telling me he was ready, that his control over his body was fierce. "Ready for me to claim you now?"

I nodded, my forehead pressing into the soft mattress.

"Good little mate. More lube. More fingers first. Then I'll get my cock in there. Claim you. Fill you with my seed."

I nodded again and he shifted slightly so he could do as he'd said. A finger slipped into me, deeper this time. It was coated liberally in lube. My mind was too muddled to figure out the logistics, but I knew I wasn't even supposed to think. My job was to feel, to submit in every way. I was doing it. I had no choice, not that he would take me there roughly or without my readiness.

And yet I could say butterfly. But I wouldn't. I wanted this. I wanted him. He was the one to protect us both, to ensure I could handle him, that my body was prepared, my mind was at ease. My body, too.

So when he'd worked two fingers, then three into my virgin ass, coating me liberally inside and out with the slick lubricant, scissoring them to open me up in preparation for his cock, I gripped the blankets, breathed through it. Gave over to it. It burned, the stretch, but my mate was slow, patient, consistently adding more and more lube.

He didn't touch my clit again, which only made me needier. I knew what it felt like to come with something in my ass, and I knew he wouldn't give it to me again until he was deep inside. He wanted to share the pleasure with me.

His fingers slipped free and immediately I felt the insistent press of his cock. Hard, yet warm and slick. The prod was insistent, yet the way he crooned praise, commands, and promises in my ear, I relaxed. Relented.

Allowed him entrance. He slipped in with a silent pop and I gasped. He was so much bigger than I remembered. Thick and the broad head was all that filled me.

"There, little mate." His voice was rough, like sandpaper. "I'm in. This ass is mine. Now let me claim it."

He moved then, slowly worked himself all the way in, the slickness of the lube easing his way. Patiently. Reverently. When his hips pressed against my bottom, I knew I'd taken all of him. I was so full and he was so deep. It was strange that this was the way I truly learned his size, that his cock was not only thick with a flared crown that hit every inch of me, but long, too.

Reaching around, he flicked my clit with his finger as he pulled back, slid in. Began to fuck me.

The play of his cock over the nerve endings around the ring of my entrance flared with each pass. It was like lightning. Like a shock of electricity. Intense and powerful, hot and bright. Jangly. Indescribable.

The submission of him claiming me like this, with him taking me from behind, was overwhelming. It was a true mating, dark and carnal. Wild and passionate. His dominance, his control was overwhelming.

"So tight. So perfect. This ass is mine. You're mine." He continued to speak these words over and over as he fucked me. I clenched and relaxed one after the other, my body not sure what to do. All it could handle was the pleasure, the need to come.

He came with a harsh growl, only after he pushed me over the edge. There was no scream this time, but a deep, guttural growl that escaped my lips. I clenched and squeezed around his cock, trying to pull it in even deeper.

Exhausted, weary, sore, I felt his seed coat my inner walls, knew I was claimed. Sweaty and breathing roughly, I clenched the blankets, felt the material abrade my nipples. Done in. Ruined, destroyed for any other male. As he said, I was his.

Yet was he mine?

5

I STOOD AROUND THE PERIMETER OF THE GATHERING chamber and watched the brides mingle with their warriors. Guardians of our most precious treasure. Not all were blessed, as I was, with a Marked Mate. Most, in fact, would need to woo their bride with kind words and wicked tongues used generously on her sweet, wet heat. As I'd done with my mate.

Even now, Helen's taste was branded into my mind, on my tongue. I could not tear my gaze from her. She wore a dark red gown today, the reflective material clinging to the curve of hips and breasts in blatant invitation.

Gods, she was beautiful. Mine. Yet not. She allowed

my touch, but did not know who I really was. My hideous face. My scars. Even now, I feared one look at me would send her away, screaming in horror. Disgusted. Her rejection would be a blow I could not survive with my soul intact. Especially after the previous night and how she'd submitted to me so beautifully. Her ass, I'd opened it up, claimed it. And I'd ensured she loved every inch of my cock I'd filled it with. Left her sated and replete, coated deep with my seed.

Helen was a miracle. Literally. A one in a hundred chance. And to have her volunteer and come from a planet on the other side of the galaxy? No, it was one in a million. Billion, even. An incredible blessing. A blessing I did not deserve, but could not find the strength to give up.

Beside me, Quinn watched with his arms crossed and an arched brow. "What is Bryn doing with that female? He's going to lose her if he doesn't stop acting like an ass."

Bryn was an Elite Hunter, as we were, and he, too, had found his Marked Mate. Like Helen, she was a human female, a woman from Earth named Katie who, even now, glared at him as if he were evil incarnate. *That* was not a look I ever wanted to see aimed at me from Helen.

"I don't know what is in his heart," I replied neutrally.

"And what of your mate?" Quinn asked.

I eyed him, seeing the way he'd segued to me. "Her second virginity is mine," I growled, remembering the tight fit of that virgin hole, the way I'd coaxed her body open, the way she'd come alive with the dark pleasure of the claiming. She'd submitted beautifully. Gasped in the surprised delight of the act and it had been my undoing. No, *she* was my undoing. Gods, I was going insane. My mate was passionate and wild, fierce and submissive. And she had a kinky side I would have to continue to discover. Restraints, especially. And the way she creamed for a spanking...*fuck.*

"And?" He looked genuinely confused. "What are you doing sulking over here with me while Hunters swarm her like an unclaimed prize?" He stuck his arm out, pointed in her direction.

I shook my head. "She is too beautiful. She will not survive the sight of me."

Quinn's golden eyes rounded in shock as he put his hands on his hips. "Are you fucking kidding me?" He leaned in so our conversation remained private. "You made her wear a blindfold? Again?"

"Yes."

"Well, Bryn's not the only idiot around here about to lose his mate." Quinn's voice was cold as ice and I felt the sting of his words.

"What are you talking about?" I watched each of the Hunters who approached my mate during this social time before the group meal. She was polite. Her smile was calm, poised, and completely uninterested. She knew she was mine. I just had to get her to fall in love with me before I revealed the truth. "She's mine."

He laughed. "Does she know that?"

"Her virgin ass does," I murmured. I was smug, but not for long, as a young Hunter named Weston bowed low over her hand and smiled, making her cheeks turn an enticing shade of pink. I'd seen that color on her flushed skin last night as I'd fucked her and when she'd come, her walls clenching and milking the cum from my balls. I'd filled her ass and made her mine. Mine!

How dare he even lay eyes upon her?

I did not like seeing that color on her face in response to another male. My hands curled into fists, wanting to stalk over and punch Weston in the fucking face. But this was my doing. My own personal torture.

The silence stretched and I watched her extract her hand from the young Hunter's with a shy smile. She stood with other Earth females I'd seen her with before. They eyed Weston, but gave him no encouragement. Beside me, Quinn grunted and hit me in the shoulder. "You better pull your stubborn head out of your ass, Zee, before you lose her."

"I am a monster," I insisted adamantly.

"If she's your Marked Mate, she won't care." He walked away, and I let him go, my complete attention on the beautiful young woman who had conquered me, who owned me, and didn't even know my name.

———

H*E WAS WATCHING ME*. S*TARING*. H*E'D BEEN STARING* since I entered the room. Zee. My mate. My beautiful, scarred warrior. I'd caught a glimpse of him from across the room and it was next to impossible not to look at him, to walk over to him, cup my hand behind his neck and pull him down for a kiss.

Just knowing his eyes were on me alone made my pussy wet, my nipples pebble into hard peaks under my dress.

The young Hunter who'd kissed the back of my hand, a handsome younger Hunter named Weston, would think the flush on my cheeks was due to his attention.

The opposite was true. I didn't care one bit about him and once he walked away—which I hoped was soon—I wouldn't remember what he looked like.

Zee's presence was burning through me like an internal blowtorch, and I had no way to push him into revealing the truth.

I watched, from the corner of my eye, as he spoke to his friend, a golden Hunter named Quinn. With his long hair and amber eyes, Quinn looked almost like a lion next to my dark-haired warrior. Quinn was perfect. Beautiful. Boring. He did not make my pulse race or my body heat. His gaze did not make my skin burn or my heart flutter in anticipation.

Only Zee made me *want.* And when he left the room, I felt the loss of his presence keenly. Quinn departed as well, but in a different direction.

I caught Katie's eye as she held court, torturing the Hunter named Bryn by flirting with every available male in the room. Lexi was nowhere to be seen, no doubt off with her lucky new mate, Von. I had yet to hear if she'd been fully claimed yet, but I imagined the next time I saw her it would be a done deed. And Dani? Poor Dani. She sat in a corner with a book, ignoring everything and everyone around her as if she were a marble statue, or a being not of this world. Her pain was a palpable thing, and I often caught Katie darting worried glances her direction as well. Males looked her way, but it was as if she had a neon sign over her head that said, "stay away." No one approached.

I'd had enough.

Pulling my hand from Weston's, I rose and excused myself, determined to track down Zee's friend, Quinn. I'd seen him leave down a side hallway and I followed. He would help me with Zee. He had to.

My pace was quick, nearly running, by the time I caught up to him several long hallways away from the main gathering room. "Quinn? May I speak with you?" I sounded breathless; I was a photographer, not an aerobics instructor.

Quinn, the lion, turned and bowed low. "My lady?"

I sensed he was surprised by my presence, but did not let it show.

My hands twisted in front of me, but I couldn't lose courage now. "Why won't Zee tell me who he is?" I blurted.

Quinn's eyebrows rose in shock. "You know his identity?"

"Of course. I'm a woman. I'm not stupid."

He straightened to his full height and looked down his nose at me as if he were a prince and I, a peasant. "Perhaps you are, indeed, stupid if you do not know the answer to the question."

My gut churned and I flushed hotly at the scolding I didn't understand. I had no idea. "I don't. Please. Just tell me. Does he not want a mate? Did he want a blonde, instead? A redhead? What? Why does he come to me every night and refuse to tell me who he is?"

He looked stunned by my outburst, and my words. "My apologies for the disrespectful tone. You truly don't know?"

I shook my head, blinked back tears. I'd held them off; I couldn't let them fall now. "No. You have to help me. Please." I wasn't above begging. Not if it would get me what I wanted. Zee. Mine. Forever.

"His scars."

"What about them?" I asked, frowning.

"What—" Quinn took a step back, his mouth half-formed around his next word. "He fears his appearance will frighten you, cause you to reject his claim."

My turn to cross my arms and glare. "That's ridiculous."

His eyes widened. "You truly don't care about his battle scars? They don't repulse you?"

Holy shit. This really was the problem? I imagined he might find them unfavorable and was afraid for me to see them, but Zee thought I'd reject him because of some stupid scars?

"I'm in love with him," I shouted, angry now for no good reason. If someone were to overhear, I didn't care. "Of course some stupid scars don't bother me." Men. He was rejecting me. Leaving me in the dark. Torturing both of us. All because of some the battle wounds that healed poorly?

Quinn raised his hands in surrender and I took a deep breath, regaining control. "My apologies if I have insulted you, my lady."

"Look, Zee is mine. I want him. And I need your help."

"Help?" His gaze darkened and the corners of his eyes crinkled with mischief. He bowed slightly. "Tell me what I might do to assist."

"I need to drive him crazy," I replied, thinking of Katie and how she'd been taunting Hunter Bryn. "Force his hand. I might be submissive, but it's time I took control. Right now, he thinks he's in charge and that's not working out so well. It's time for me to take over. To push him, just as he pushes me." I met Quinn's gaze and tried to force every bit of determination I had to shine from my eyes.

"So, your plan is to enrage him?" He stroked his

chin as he spoke, mulling over my words. "Make him jealous so he'll have to intervene?"

I nodded once. "Exactly."

It felt dangerous. Naughty. Worse than the see-through blindfold. And I couldn't wait to get started. I'd see just how far my new master could be pushed.

Quinn's chuckle made me smile in response. "You are aware of the consequences to your…um, bare ass."

I smiled at the Hunter, and while I could feel my blush, I didn't care if he knew I was definitely getting spanked for topping from the bottom. Oh, I so was. "Yes."

"Very well. I am at your disposal."

———

ZEE, TWELVE HOURS LATER

I WAS GOING TO KILL HIM.

Slowly.

I'd rip his body in half with my bare hands and smash his skull into pulp on the stone pillars of the Touchstone.

In exactly seven minutes, my shift was over. My duty, to guard the brides this day, done.

And then I no longer needed to remain watchful from my post. I would kill the man who'd dared lie to my mate.

69

Even now as I eyed her closely, Helen laughed, her head thrown back with joy as she talked to the other brides. "Oh, my god! I found him. He told me everything."

One of the brides, a very small female from Earth named Dani, jumped to her feet and gave my mate a hug. "Details. We need details."

"His name is Quinn. I'll tell you more...all of it," Helen promised as my blood boiled.

I stilled. Quinn? My friend, Quinn? Ex-friend. What the fuck was he doing with Helen? And she thinks *he's* her Marked Mate? The one whose palm burned for her? The one who came to her in her dreams? Who ate her sweet pussy until she came all over his face? Who opened up her tight ass with his cock and made her come?

Quinn was going to die a slow...painful... excruciating death. And I was going to enjoy every minute of it.

"But I can't right now," Helen continued. "I'm meeting him again. Maybe this time he'll take my third virginity. I'm so excited for that big cock, to have it deep inside of me. *Finally.* I have to hurry."

"You go, girl," Katie chuckled, waggling her eyebrows, and Helen twirled in her clinging red gown. She looked so thrilled—ecstatic—to go to him. To go to Quinn, the fucker. To have him *fuck* her.

No. Fucking. Way.

"I used that rose perfume you gave me," she

whispered, although her soft voice carried to me. "I hope he likes it. I put it *everywhere.*"

She blushed as her gaze darted to me, just for a moment, not as if she assumed I was her mate, but as if she were worried about a random male overhearing her statement.

Rose perfume? *Everywhere?* I did not know what a rose smelled like, but if it made Helen's cheeks so flushed with excitement, I would discover soon enough. I stepped closer to her. Bowed.

"Do you require an escort, my lady?" My voice was gravelly. Deep. Filled with barely suppressed rage. Not at her. Never at her. But at the male who dared to try to seduce her in my stead, knowing, *knowing* she was mine. To take what belonged to me. He was deceiving her, and me. Quinn would not touch a hair on her head let alone one inch of her silky skin. Or get his cock anywhere near her pussy.

My heart nearly stopped beating, cold dread filling my veins, at the dreamy look on Helen's face when she turned to answer me. "Oh, no, thank you. He's so... sexy. So charming. So dominant."

She gave me a look as if she were having an orgasm right then and there. My cock swelled painfully against the front of my pants. I'd brought her pleasure many times, but I had yet to see her eyes as I did so. The fucking blindfold. Dammit. I clenched my hands into fists.

She held up her hand, palm out, so I could see her

mark. The mark that pulsed in tune to *my* mark on *my* palm. Not Quinn's.

"He's my mate, I just know it. I'll be fine. Thank you."

My hands clenched into fists and I broke the wooden railing I leaned against, splinters slicing their way into the flesh of my palm. The pain brought me back to myself as I watched my mate walk away, humming. Happy. Hips swaying seductively.

I checked the time. Five minutes.

Fuck that.

I raced after her, through the doorway she'd just passed. But when I entered the corridor, she was nowhere to be seen.

Two Hunters stood guard at the entrance. I approached. "Did you see a bride in red? Brown hair? She just exited through these doors?"

They looked at each other. One shrugged as if my mate's future, her body, the Hunter most likely touching her right now, was of no concern.

I shoved him against the wall, a snarl in my voice and death in my eyes. "Where. Did. She. Go?"

"She's with her mate," he answered, his eyes wide in surprise.

"*I'm her mate*," I hissed through clenched teeth.

"Gods, Zee. Relax." The other guard leaned his shoulder against the wall, feet crossed as if he didn't have a care in the world. As if I wasn't threatening to murder his companion.

I shook the man in front of me. "I'll ask one more time. Where is she?"

He tilted his head further down the hallway. "She was headed for the private quarters."

"With who? Quinn?" I gritted out my friend's name through clenched teeth.

"Didn't see his face." He was lying. I could see it in his eyes, but I didn't need him to tell me. If I'd been using my head, I would have realized that the only thing I was doing here was wasting my time.

Releasing the guard, I turned and strode away, letting the thing inside me, the Hunter, take over.

Scents danced on the air. Including hers. Sweet. Unique. The flowery scent of her perfume—rose—like a beacon. I followed it to the private quarters. Confused when the scent ended abruptly in an unclaimed room.

Any Hunter here, myself included, would have taken her to his private room for a final claiming, for once a cock was buried deep in a sweet pussy, he wasn't letting her up from the bed for a long, long time. Using an empty, unassigned room didn't make any sense.

Yet her scent led me here.

As did the voices on the other side of the door.

Hers. His.

My ears flooded with the pounding of my pulse and all I could see was his hands on her. Touching her. Fucking her. Claiming what was mine. Quinn was a dead man. And my mate? She would discover the one who ruled her body. The only one who could bring her pleasure because I knew every inch of her. Every gasp of pleasure, clench of desire, gush of arousal. Her fucking taste. It was all mine.

And I was taking it. Now.

$\mathcal{H}$elen

QUINN LEANED AGAINST THE WALL, ARMS CROSSED. THE bed loomed large between us. Untouched. He was on the other side of the room, nowhere near me, for while we'd intentionally riled Zee, hopefully to the breaking point, he'd said he didn't want to get hurt. Or die.

I knew Zee was a possessive mate and when the door flew open, slamming against the wall and bouncing off, I knew Quinn's measures for personal safety were reasonable.

Zee was all but resonating with anger. His muscles were taut with it, his square jaw clenched. His breathing was ragged, his fists clenched. Handsome in his anger. And the knowledge that I'd made him this way made me feel so powerful.

His head swiveled from Quinn to me. His eyes, so dark, burned with intensity.

I swallowed, my mouth suddenly dry. I wanted to drop to my knees before him, to wait for his command, to feel all of this power unleashed on me.

While he was practically unbridled in his anger, I knew he would never harm me. He'd turn all this wicked energy into the final claiming. My pussy ached and my nipples hardened beneath my gown at the possibility.

"Are you unharmed?" he asked.

I nodded, licked my lips. "I'm fine."

"Good." He turned away from me so I could see the hard lines of his back, the taut curves of his butt. "You, *friend*, will not be so lucky."

Quinn grinned and held his hands up, as if in surrender. "What's the matter, Zee?"

Zee took one step closer as if prowling his prey. "You dare to claim my mate?"

Quinn shrugged. "You haven't done so."

I watched the exchange, my breath held.

"I have. I've claimed her mouth, her ass. *She's mine and you fucking know it.*" While Zee still faced his friend, he reached his arm back, pointed at me.

I was embarrassed, the two friends speaking of me so intimately, and yet as if I weren't in the room.

"Then why doesn't she know that?" Quinn asked.

"Because—" Zee didn't finish because he realized then what he'd done. How he'd given himself away.

Quinn stepped up to Zee, slapped him on the shoulder. "My work here is done. My lady." The Hunter bowed to me before leaving the room, closing the door behind him.

Zee hadn't moved, didn't turn to look at me.

The only thing I could hear was his ragged breathing and the frantic beat of my heart.

"Master," I whispered.

He flinched, the subtle ripple of his muscles bunching his shoulders. He still didn't move.

I walked around so I stood before him. My eyes were uncovered. My head was lifted, my gaze on him. *On him.* On his face. His scars.

"Master, I see you. I saw you in the other room when you spoke with me. I saw you when you asked me if I was fine. I see you now. I haven't flinched, haven't been repulsed. I *want* to see you."

His eyes blazed with fury, a vein pulsed at his temple.

"No. Don't look."

The grating words were a knife to my heart.

"I can't look away," I replied.

Slowly, carefully, I lifted my hand toward his face.

He leaned back slightly, but I didn't relent. With my fingertips, I touched the red, raised skin. A breath hissed between his closed lips.

"I *see* you," I repeated. "I *want* you."

"Why?" he growled, stepping back as if the touch burned him.

"You are my mate. The only one in the universe for me. The testing has never been wrong. Neither has a mark."

"No." He shook his head.

I was determined to get through to this hard-headed warrior. "Are you telling me it wasn't you who touched me in my dreams? That the mark on your palm isn't throbbing right now to touch me? That it wasn't your commands that had me on my knees? Had me bent over the bed to take your cock in my virgin ass?"

"Why?" he repeated, although I saw heat mix with the anger in his gaze. "Why would you want me?"

"Why wouldn't I?"

I stepped forward then, closed the distance between us. Pressed my body against him, my hands cupping the sides of his head. I had to go up on tiptoe to do so, he was so big.

"Look at me," he said, his voice rough with pain.

"I am. I don't see scars. I see badges of survival. Of honor. I see the mate who's captured my heart. Who's in my soul. Who's done things to me only a mate can. Who I love."

His eyes narrowed and his hands came up to cover mine.

"You are too beautiful, Helen. You should want Quinn. If I were a female, I would find him appealing."

His words made me laugh. Zee? A female? He was so virile, so male, the idea was ridiculous. And that big cock he wielded between his legs? Pure male perfection.

"I don't want Quinn. I want you. I've only wanted you. While you are listening, you are not hearing me."

"Mate," I heard the warning tone of his voice and I shuddered. My nipples were almost painfully hard. "Careful what you say to me. Did you lure me here under false pretenses? Recruit my friend and fellow Hunter into your scheme?"

I wouldn't deny the truth.

"I want you, Hunter Zee." My hand came up to the clasp on my dress and I undid it as I continued. "My mark aches for you. My pussy aches for you." The gauzy fabric slid down my body and pooled at my feet. I stepped from the circle of fabric and then dropped to my knees. Instead of lowering my eyes, I kept them fixed on his, my chin titled up. "Claim me, Master. Make me yours forever."

His gaze roamed my body. I'd dressed with care, wearing ruby red garters and stockings this time. My breasts spilled from the top of the red, demi-cut lace bra and the G-string I wore was completely translucent, embroidered with red roses. Translucent not only because of the fabric, but my copious need for him. Even my shoes were made for sin, with four-inch spiked heels. Katie had let me use some bright red toenail polish. I looked like a vixen, like a woman I hardly knew. But I wanted to be this…for him. I wanted to drive him crazy. Out of his mind.

I wanted to be his.

When he held his hand out to me and helped me stand, to lead me to the bed, I eagerly followed, sure that I had won. That I was about to get exactly what I wanted.

Alarm bells didn't start to ring until he sat and pulled me down to lay, face down, over his lap. My head was close to the floor on one side of his bent legs, my toes barely touching on the other.

"You lied to me. You misled me. You caused me to feel rage at a friend and worry for your safety."

His palm came to rest on my bare bottom, exposed by the scant covering of the G-string underwear. "I'm sorry. I had to. You wouldn't tell me who you were."

As his palm petted my backside with the softest caress, I realized my mistake. This was his game. His rules. If I really wanted him to be my master, if I really wanted to serve him, I should have waited. I was impatient. Selfish, especially since it had taken such a ruse to get him to give over to the truth.

"I warned you, mate, what would happen if you lied to me or deceived me about your needs." His hand landed on my bare bottom with a sharp sting and I gasped as he spanked me again and again. The sting was sharp, but it morphed, spreading to tingly pleasure throughout my body. "Why did you lie to me?"

Every second his hand swatted my bottom, over

and over, it left a growing heat behind as the truth built up inside me like a volcano about to erupt. The fire spread, and my pussy was wetter than it had ever been, the ache there becoming acutely painful as my arousal grew. "I...I didn't feel safe. I needed to know you were going to claim me, Master. I didn't feel safe."

The truth burst from me on a sob and his hand stilled immediately.

"Helen." There was agony in his voice, and I felt even worse for causing him more pain.

"Please, Master, I was weak. It's my fault. I should have waited for you to be ready. It wasn't my place."

"No, love," he all but groaned. "It's my fault. I was a coward. So many have rejected me, feared me because of the scars. I should have believed in the mark, in the power of our match. In you."

I slid from his lap and knelt on the floor before him, my body between his parted knees, looking up into his eyes. The darkness there was edged with regret and pain. I could not allow either. It was over. The truth was out. There was nothing between us now. Perhaps only my G-string. "Master, please, may I kiss you now?"

His hand reached out and cupped the side of my face. "Of course. I am yours, Helen. Body and soul. I will give you anything you need."

Remaining on my knees, I leaned my face into his touch, hungry for more. But I had a plan in mind now, and I couldn't stop thinking about it. "May I remove your clothes, Master?"

He nodded and I rose. I started with his shirt, pulling it off over his head. I leaned forward and traced every scar, every inch of him with lips and tongue and teeth. *This* is what I'd been waiting for. What I needed, for him to know I would not ignore this part of him.

Zee held himself rigid as I explored; his hands fisted at his sides on the bed as I worked my way down his abdomen to his waist. Making quick work of the clasp, he lifted his hips off the bed to assist me as I yanked his pants down. When he was gloriously naked, I stepped back and admired what was mine.

"You are beautiful, Master."

His gaze was on my breasts. My stomach. The dark red scrap of fabric covering my sex. "Have you taken what you need, mate?"

Slowly, I shook my head. "No. Not yet." There was no way. I wasn't finished with him. I knew as soon as I admitted I was feeling better, secure, he would take control again and I'd lose my opportunity to touch him. Learn him.

Slowly, to tease him, I worked the scrap of lace down over my hips and off, kicking the miniscule garment aside. Reaching behind me, I released my bra and slid it down my arms as well so I stood before him in garters, stockings, and high heels.

His huge, rigid cock surged toward me as if it had a mind of its own and I laughed, pleased that his pulse raced at the base of his neck, his breathing hitched. His hands clenched into fists, his knuckles white against the blanket covering the bed.

Without warning, I dropped to my knees once again and took him into my mouth, swallowing him down, sucking, licking, driving him mad until his hand fisted in my hair and he forced me to release him. I'd taken him deep before, but this time I could see every pulsing inch, put my hands on his thighs.

"Enough."

"Not enough." I held his gaze as I climbed onto his lap, my knees straddling either side of his waist and resting on the bed beside him. I settled with his cock at the entrance of my virgin pussy. I was so close I could see the dark color of his eyes, the stubble of his jaw, the slight crook to his nose. "I want you inside me, Zee. I want you to be mine. Forever."

"Gods, Helen." His dark eyes flared. "Yes. You are mine."

I kissed him as I slid down onto his hard length, taking him slowly into my pussy. My body was ready for him, all but dripping with my arousal. I ignored the burn, the pain as he stretched me, filling me for the first time. I pressed down, wiggling and moving until he finally bottomed out inside me. Until he was mine. "I'm claiming you, Hunter Zee. I claim you. You're mine now." I whispered the words against his neck, against the very scars that had nearly kept this wonderful warrior from me. I breathed in his scent, licked his hot skin.

With a groan, he shifted, lifting me and twisting us both so that he came down on top of me on the bed. We faced one another, and he took my hand, palm to palm, mark to mark as heat burned through me. This was it. The claiming. There was no going back for either of us. I welcomed the heat, the pulsing pleasure that rushed through my body. Only he could do this to me. My Marked Mate. He gazed into my eyes as he began to move. In. Out. Slowly. So slowly I thought I would die from pleasure. This was fucking. Making love. Passionate. Dark. Freeing. Lovely.

I pulled his head to mine with my free hand, kissing him with all the love I felt bursting through me as he reached between us to stroke my clit.

My pussy went into spasms and I arched against him, crying out as I exploded, milking his cock as he followed me over the edge.

He didn't move for a long while and I held him, his forehead pressed to mine as I stroked his back, his sides. His scars. He was fierce and strong and mine.

"I love you, Master."

"And I love you, mate."

"Forever?" I asked, even though my pride demanded I hold my tongue.

"Beyond death, Helen. I'll never let you go."

And that was exactly what I wanted to hear. So I kissed him again.

And again.

And again.

Until his cock grew thicker and longer inside me. His control had snapped, his need too great for him to last. I didn't mind because this was the most amazing pleasure ever. I'd loved the way he'd taken my mouth, the way he'd fucked my ass. But this...god, this was everything. We were one, joined and connected in the most elemental of ways. And the mark, the heat of our two touching, almost seared my skin. He moaned my name as he came, and he took me with him. I milked every drop from him, took his seed into my body.

And all at once, the marks went silent. The pulsing was gone. The heat was now only in my pussy. The mark had brought us together and was no longer needed. The claim was complete.

"The first time was too quick," he said once he caught his breath. "Yet you are no longer in control. I gave you the power you wanted, but it is mine once again. Do I need to tie you up, mate?"

I grinned up at him, thrilled he was finally mine. Body and soul.

"Yes, please."

———

Ready for more? Read His Virgin Bride next!

After a life on the streets, Katie chooses the Interstellar

Brides Program for a chance at a new life, a new identity. But when she arrives on Everis, her Marked Mate refuses to claim her. As an Elite Hunter, Bryn has to travel to Hyperion, a known world of gangs and vicious evil to bring an assassin to justice, and leave her behind.

She might be innocent in body, but Katie knows her honorable mate is walking into a foreign world, a world she knows all too well. If she must seduce him, she will. If she must steal away on his ship and follow him to another world, she will. And if she must seduce the sexy-as-sin leader of the criminal legions they meet to save her mate? Well then, her innocence is a weapon, and she's not afraid to use it.

Click here to get His Virgin Bride now!

A SPECIAL THANK YOU TO MY READERS...

Want more? I've got **hidden** bonus content on my web site *exclusively* for those on my mailing list.

If you are already on my email list, you don't need to do a thing! Simply scroll to the bottom of my newsletter emails and click on the ***super-secret*** link.

Not a member? What are you waiting for? In addition to ALL of my bonus content (great new stuff will be added regularly) you will be the first to hear about my newest release the second it hits the stores—AND you will get a free book as a special welcome gift.

Sign up now! http://freescifiromance.com

FIND YOUR INTERSTELLAR MATCH!

YOUR mate is out there. Take the test today and discover your perfect match. Are you ready for a sexy alien mate (or two)?

VOLUNTEER NOW!

interstellarbridesprogram.com

DO YOU LOVE AUDIOBOOKS?

Grace Goodwin's books are now available as audiobooks…everywhere.

LET'S TALK SPOILER ROOM!

Interested in joining my **Sci-Fi Squad**? Meet new like-minded sci-fi romance fanatics and chat with Grace! Get excerpts, cover reveals and sneak peeks before anyone else. Be part of a private Facebook group that shares pictures and fun news! Join here:

https://www.facebook.com/groups/scifisquad/

***

Want to talk about Grace Goodwin books with others? Join the **SPOILER ROOM** and spoil away! Your GG BFFs are waiting! (And so is Grace)

Join here:

https://www.facebook.com/groups/ggspoilerroom/

GET A FREE BOOK!

JOIN MY MAILING LIST TO BE THE FIRST TO KNOW OF NEW RELEASES, FREE BOOKS, SPECIAL PRICES AND OTHER AUTHOR GIVEAWAYS.

http://freescifiromance.com

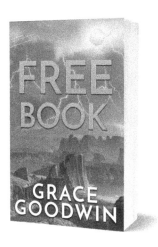

ALSO BY GRACE GOODWIN

Other Books

ABOUT GRACE

Grace Goodwin is a USA Today and international bestselling author of Sci-Fi and Paranormal romance with more than one million books sold. Grace's titles are available worldwide in multiple languages in ebook, print and audio formats. Two best friends, one left-brained, the other right-brained, make up the award-winning writing duo that is Grace Goodwin.

They are both mothers, escape room enthusiasts, avid readers and intrepid defenders of their preferred beverages. (There may or may not be an ongoing tea vs. coffee war occurring during their daily communications.) Grace loves to hear from readers!

All of Grace's books can be read as sexy, stand-alone adventures. But be careful, she likes her heroes hot and her love scenes hotter. You have been warned...

www.gracegoodwin.com
gracegoodwinauthor@gmail.com

9 781795 901703